SUPER SOCCER BOY

AND THE ALIEN INVASION

BY JUDY BROWN

Piccadilly Press • London

First published in Great Britain in 2011 by
Piccadilly Press Ltd, 5 Castle Road, London NW1 8PR
www.piccadillypress.co.uk

ISBN: 978 1 84812 136 2

1 3 5 7 9 10 8 6 4 2

Printed in the UK by CPI Bookmarque,
Croydon, CR0 4TD
Cover design by Simon Davis
Cover illustration by Judy Brown
Text design by Simon Davis

Chapter One

Tournament Time

'Who wants another sausage?' asked Mr Blunt.

A chorus of 'me's' rang out as dozens of hungry Little League footballers charged towards him. Not surprisingly Harry Gribble, also known as Super Soccer Boy, got there first.

'Thank you, Mr B,' said Harry as he shoved a steaming sausage into a bun and smothered it in mustard and tomato ketchup.

It was the beginning of the summer holidays and Harry's Little League team was on its first ever football tour in Puddletown-on-Sea. His dad, as manager, should have been there, but he'd broken his ankle the week before playing football for his Sunday League team. One of Harry's teachers, Mr Blunt, had stepped in at the

last moment. He knew most of the team anyway as they played for the school team.

The organisers had arranged a big welcome barbecue for all the players and coaches and Mr Blunt was in charge of the sausages. Harry's team, the Middletown Mini-Stars, had played the first game of the tournament that afternoon and after a stunning eighteen-one victory, they were ready to stuff their faces. The amazing score was, of course, down to Harry. He had been useless at football until fairly recently, when a freak lightning bolt had transformed him from 'Harry Gribble who couldn't even dribble,' into Super Soccer Boy. He now had brilliant football skills and was a crucial member of the team.

'These sausages are awesome,' said Jake. He sat down on the wall next to where Harry was sitting. Ron, Harry's pet rat, popped his head out of Harry's hoody and sniffed the sausagey aroma. Harry picked a bit off and gave it to Ron who gobbled it down hungrily.

Jake grinned. 'I thought you were supposed to leave him at home,' he said, spraying Harry with bits of sausage as he spoke.

'I know,' said Harry, 'but he looked so sad when I was packing that I just couldn't leave him behind. No one'll notice.'

'Attention!' called one of the organisers. He banged two saucepan lids together until everyone was quiet. 'I would like to introduce the mayor of Puddletown, who is going to say a few words.'

'This'll be boring,' whispered Jake.

A little fat man with a bald head and a gold

chain round his neck stepped forward.

'Ahem. I would like to welcome you all here to our annual Little League Tournament. I know things have kicked off – heh, heh, just my little joke – to a fabulous start this afternoon with the, er . . .' He looked at a piece of paper. '. . . Middletown Mini-Stars scoring an impressive eighteen goals in their first match.'

Harry's team mates proudly patted him on the back.

'I'm sure many more goals will be scored by all the teams. So let us look forward to a great tournament and good luck to everyone!'

Just as the mayor finished speaking, a flash of light whooshed across the sky behind him.

'Wow! Fireworks!' said Eddie, one of the Mini-stars' mid-fielders.

'That's impressive,' said Jake. 'I'm amazed they think we're important enough for fireworks.'

Whoooooosh! There was another flash.

'Oooooooo!' went the crowd of children and adults. There was a round of applause.

The organisers looked puzzled though.

'That was no firework,' said Harry.

Whooooosh! Whoooosh! Whooooooooshhh! Three flashes came together.

'What is it then?' asked Jake.

'Meteors, I think,' said Harry. 'It's a meteor shower.'

Some of the other people watching had come

to the same conclusion.

'It must be a sign,' someone said. 'It's obviously going to be a special tournament.'

'It's odd,' said Harry. 'I don't remember hearing anything about a meteor shower being forecast.' He stared into the sky. Something seemed strange, but he couldn't quite work out what it was.

'It's so cool,' said Jake, trying unsuccessfully, like many of the others, to take a picture on his phone.

'Talking of cool,' said Harry, 'I'm suddenly feeling a bit cold.' He shivered.

'Yeah, me too,' said Jake, zipping up his jacket. 'Let's go and get some more food.'

Chapter Two

Meteor Mystery

The next morning, Harry and his team woke up in their hotel to brilliant sunshine.

Mr Blunt was in the corridor marching up and down and knocking on the bedroom doors. 'Everybody downstairs for breakfast,' he said.

Harry and Jake were sharing a room with Eddie and Will. Ten minutes later, after a battle to get into the bathroom first, they all went to the dining room.

'Hurry up, you boys,' said Mr Blunt. 'I was just telling everyone to bring swimming stuff with them to the match. Then we can have a dip in the sea to cool off afterwards. The pitch is right next to the beach.'

It sounded like a great plan. With the sun shining through the big glass windows in the dining room it felt like they were in a greenhouse. If they were hot now, they'd be really hot after the game.

Harry managed to sneak some breakfast up to Ron and then packed his football kit, towel and swimming shorts.

They were ready early so the team waited in the hotel lounge. The TV was on and a news reporter was interviewing some scientist about the previous night's unexpected meteor shower.

'So, Professor Winklestein, can you tell us anything about last night's spectacular display?'

'Not really, Eamonn, no,' said the professor. 'It came quite literally "out of the blue" as they say! Ha ha.'

'Er, yes, most curious, Professor. Will we get any more of these unexpected meteor showers?'

'Well, if I could tell you that then they

wouldn't be unexpected, now, would they? Ha ha! Who knows, Eamonn? Nature is a very mysterious thing.'

'Indeed it is. Thank you, Professor.'

'He was helpful,' said Jake, 'eh, Harry?'

Harry was clearly miles away.

'Harry?' Jake felt anxious – he'd seen that look on Harry's face before. It always meant trouble was brewing.

'What . . .? Oh yes. I was just thinking about

the meteors last night. There was something odd about them, but I couldn't quite think what it was at the time.'

'But now you can?' asked Jake.

'You know, I think I can,' Harry said, dreamily.

'And?'

'I could swear they were falling in formation. You know – as if they were all the same distance apart.'

'Freaky,' said Jake.

More than freaky, thought Harry.

Just then, Mr Blunt came in. 'OK, lads, everybody got their kit together? Let's go play football!'

They all followed Mr Blunt to the hotel foyer. As he opened the door, a blast of cold air hit their faces.

'Cor!' said Mr Blunt. 'That's one chilly sea breeze.'

Meanwhile out at sea . . .

THE ZIGLONS OF PLANET ZOG, HAD LANDED THE NIGHT BEFORE. THE EMPEROR IN THE MOTHER SHIP WAS ACCOMPANIED BY A FLEET OF SMALLER CRAFT.

NOW THEY LAY DEEP BELOW THE SEA...

Chapter Three

A Chill in the Air

The Middletown Mini-Stars chatted happily to each other as they walked to the beach. Despite the clear blue sky though, it wasn't as hot outside as everyone had expected and there was definitely a strong sea breeze, like Mr Blunt had said.

'I wish I'd brought my jacket,' said Eddie. 'It's well cold this morning.'

'Don't be a wimp, Eddie. You'll warm up as soon as you get on the pitch,' said Mr Blunt. 'Sea air is good for you. Anyway, it'll be really warm later on – it's summer!'

By the time they'd got to the bottom of the hill, everybody had warmed up a bit and they were raring to go.

'Right, lads,' said Mr Blunt before the match started. 'Just do what I know you can do and we'll win this one easily. Harry, I want you in goal for the first half so Sanjay has a chance of going up front.'

'OK, Mr Blunt,' said Harry.

'Is it my imagination or is it getting colder?' said Sanjay, as they waited for the game to start. 'I've got goose pimples.'

'Me too – that sea breeze is freezing,' said Eddie.

Peeeep! The whistle blew and Middletown Mini-Stars kicked off. With Harry in goal for the first half, it was quite a tight match. The other team, the Raynes Park Rangers, were top of their own league, just like Harry's team was, and they had several chances to score. Unfortunately for them though, Harry stopped every single ball.

The second half was a completely different story. Harry played up front and dominated it from the start. His fancy footwork and super speed were too much for the Rangers and when the final whistle blew, it was another big victory – ten-nil – for the Middletown Mini-Stars.

'Well played, everyone!' said Mr Blunt. 'OK – in the sea for a splash, then packed lunch and drinks on the beach.'

After charging around a football pitch, a dip in the sea sounded good to the now pretty sweaty Middletown Mini-Stars, despite the annoyingly chilly breeze. They put on their swimming stuff in the changing rooms and set off towards the lovely, sandy beach to find a good spot for lunch where they could leave their things while they swam.

That wasn't difficult. The beach was almost deserted.

'It's very quiet down here,' said Harry, surprised.

'P'raps there's something on in town,' said Eddie. 'Or maybe everyone's in the amusement arcade.'

'Maybe . . .' said Harry. He looked out to sea. Not a single person was swimming.

'OK. Who's going in for a paddle?' said Mr
Blunt, taking off his shoes and socks. Nobody
looked terribly enthusiastic.

'Come on, you babies,' he said. 'Afraid of a
little cold water, are you?' Nobody moved.
'You're all a bunch of chickens!' said Mr Blunt.
'You can't come all this way and not get your
feet wet. Last one in the sea's a great big girl with
frilly knickers.'

Reluctantly, the team began to take off their own socks and shoes. They knew that they would never hear the end of it if they wimped out.

'Let's do it together,' said Harry. 'Just go for it and charge in. What d'you think? It's the first few seconds that are always the worst, then you get used to it.'

'Erm . . . OK,' said Jake.

'S'pose so,' said Sanjay and Eddie.

The rest of them nodded in agreement. When everyone was ready to go they stood in a line.

'Let's link arms so no one can chicken out,' suggested Jake.

'Good idea!' said Harry. 'OK, is everybody ready?'

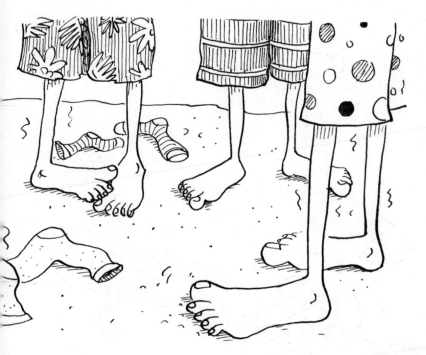

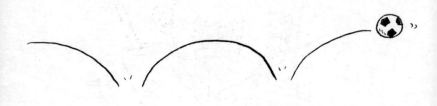

Chapter Four

Brrrrrrrrr!

'GERONIMO!!!!!!'

The entire Middletown Mini-Stars team charged down the beach towards the sea. They passed Mr Blunt on the way, almost knocking him over.

Seconds later, they entered the sea in one almighty wave.

SPPLLLLLAAAAASSSHHHH!!!!

It was *not* a pleasant experience.

'Aaaaaargh! It's COLD!!'

'Freeeeezing,' said Jake, his teeth chattering so hard he though they might break.

'I'm off,' yelled Eddie.

'Me too,' said Will.

'And m-m-me,' said Sanjay, shivering.

There was a stampede as they all turned and ran back out of the sea, even faster than they ran in. All except for Harry that is.

'Harry!' shouted Jake. 'What on Earth are you doing? You'll freeze!'

'OK, coming,' said Harry absent-mindedly. The sea was freezing cold it was true, but Harry was distracted by what he could see far away. Maybe his super soccer powers were protecting him from the cold a bit too – after all, football players have to play in freezing conditions in the middle of winter.

Harry squinted his super soccer eyes and peered at the horizon. It may have been an optical illusion, but he was almost sure he could see a sheet of ice in the distance. The sun was definitely reflecting off something. He also thought he could see little blocks of ice floating in the sea, the sun sparkling and glinting off their surfaces as they bobbed up and down.

'It can't be that cold!' said Mr Blunt as everyone raced out of the water. 'The sun's been shining on it all morning.' He dipped a toe in the sea to see what all the fuss was about. He didn't leave it there for long! 'HARRY!' he shouted. 'Come out of there right now or you'll turn blue!'

The tide had been coming in and the water was now just above Harry's knees. He took one last look at the horizon as the tip of his nose began to dribble with the cold. 'Weird,' he said, and waded back to shore.

'Harry, are you OK?' asked Jake. 'You look really peculiar.'

'Wouldn't you if you'd been standing in icy water for that long?' said Mr Blunt, putting a towel round Harry. 'I don't know what you think you were doing. You need to look after those legs of yours — they're valuable! No frostbite, I hope.'

'No, I'm fine, really,' said Harry. 'But there's something wrong with the sea. It looks as if it's started to freeze.'

'Now come on, Harry, don't exaggerate,' said

Mr Blunt, slightly worried that the cold had begun to make Harry hallucinate. 'I'm sure it's just the sun shining on the sea. Sea doesn't even freeze here in the winter – it's not the Antarctic, lad.' He laughed over-enthusiastically and patted Harry on the back.

'Perhaps it's global warming, Mr Blunt,' said Will. 'They keep saying our climate's going to change and my mum said it might actually get colder in England.'

Everyone nodded agreement. Some of them seemed scared.

'Now look,' said Mr Blunt. 'I'm sure there's nothing to worry about right now, eh, Harry?' He looked at Harry and smiled.

'Er, no, Mr Blunt. I'm sure everything's fine. Probably just a trick of the light . . . or something,' said Harry.

'OK then. Let's go back to the hotel with our packed lunches – I think there's a match on TV. Come on, everybody,' he said cheerily.

Jake walked back with Harry. 'Something's going on, isn't it, Harry?'

'Yes, Jake, I think so. I just don't know what.'

Another blast of icy air blew into shore and they both shivered.

'I hope there's something tasty in our packed lunch – I'm starving,' said Jake.

No change there then, thought Harry.

Chapter Five

An Early Night

They all settled down to watch the match on TV. The local news was just finishing with a weather report.

'Unseasonably cold weather emptied the sea and beaches of holiday-makers today,' said the newsreader. 'Forecasters are puzzled as to what is causing the sudden drop in temperature, since there is high pressure all over the country. A team of expert climatologists are on their way to the Puddletown Bay area to investigate.'

Harry was too preoccupied to enjoy the match properly. At half time he went up to his room to give Ron some scraps from lunch.

'Hi, Ron,' said Harry.

Ron jumped onto Harry's lap. 'There's definitely something odd going on down at the sea, and you and I are going to find out what it is.'

Ron was munching on what was left of Harry's apple. He looked up at him.

'We'll have to wait until everyone's asleep though.'

Just then, Jake came in. 'Hey, Harry, we're going to have a kickabout before dinner. Coming?'

'Why not?' said Harry. 'Sounds like a good plan.'

They spent the rest of the afternoon playing five-a-side, with Harry swapping teams every so often, to keep it fair. For dinner, it was a fairly unthrilling spag bol, but to the bunch of hungry footballers it was just right.

There was ice-cream (two flavours) for dessert, before they bundled back into the TV room to watch *Doctor Who*. As another programme started, it looked like everyone was happy to stay in front of the TV all evening. Harry just wanted everyone to go to bed so that he could sneak out to investigate.

Yawwn! 'I'm sooo tired,' he said dramatically, so everyone could hear. Well, you know how

yawns are catching – he thought he'd start them off. *Yawn!* 'I'm really looking forward to a good night's sleep after all that exercise.'

'You feeling all right, Harry?' asked Jake. Harry was usually the last to fall asleep.

'Fine,' – *yawn* – 'just ready for bed I guess.'

'Now you mention it – *yawn* – I'm pretty tired too,' said Sanjay.

'And me,' Eddie joined in. 'Didn't realise I was so tired.'

'Early game in the morning too,' said Harry, stretching. *Yawn.* 'What time do we have to get up, Mr B?'

'Well, Harry . . .' *Yawn.* It was working on Mr Blunt as well! 'You need to be at breakfast by eight o'clock, kick off's at ten.'

'Really! That early! I'm off to bed now, then,' said Harry.

'But it's only half-past eight,' said Jake.

'Oh well,' said Harry. 'I need my beauty sleep.

Anyway, I want to be sure I can score as many goals as possible tomorrow.' He yawned once more, just for effect.

Now everybody was yawning, including Jake. Suddenly sleep seemed like a really good idea to all of them. By nine-thirty, the Middletown Mini-Stars were tucked up in bed. The owners of the Puddletown Hotel had never seen anything like it in all their years of having Little League guests.

'What a lovely quiet bunch they are, bless 'em,' said Mrs Plunkett, the manager. 'I think I'll give 'em all an extra egg for breakfast.'

Harry had sneaked into bed fully dressed when no one was looking. When he was sure everyone else was asleep, he slipped silently out of bed. He packed a football into his backpack (you never know when you might need one, especially if you're Super Soccer Boy), and popped Ron in after it. He was just heading for the door when Jake opened one eye and spotted him.

'Where are you going?' he whispered.

'I'm going down to the beach to find out what's happening. I'm sure there's something out there in the sea – something that's making it so cold,' said Harry.

'I knew you were up to something! Wait for me then,' said Jake, jumping out of the top bunk, still dressed in his jeans and T-shirt. He knew Harry well!

Harry and Jake slipped out of the door and sped along the corridor and down the stairs as swiftly and quietly as they could.

Harry opened the front door and an icy gust blew into the hotel. In the kitchen at the end of the hallway, Mrs Plunkett shivered and buttoned up her cardigan.

'Brrrrr!' said Jake. 'It feels like winter! What's going on?'

Chapter Six

Sea of Ice

It really did feel like winter. There was even a layer of frost forming on the cars parked in the street. Harry was beginning to wish he'd worn two jumpers, but then he realised he'd only packed one. It was summer after all — why would he have needed two?

'Come on,' said Harry, his breath clearly visible in the icy air. 'Let's get moving so we warm up.' They jogged down the hill to the beach.

'What do you think it's all about, Harry?' asked Jake.

'I think it's got something to do with those meteors last night. Although I'm not sure now that they were meteors.'

'What else could they have been?' said Jake.

'That's what we're going to find out,' replied Harry. He stopped suddenly as they reached the promenade and pointed out to sea. 'Look! I was right when I said the sea was freezing over.'

The sea was full of small icebergs floating towards the shore. The ones nearest to them were only about ten or fifteen centimetres across, but the further out you looked, the bigger they got. Confused seagulls were perched on some of them.

With his amazing vision, Harry could see that the sea was almost entirely frozen. In the distance, he could just make out something on the ice.

'What's that?' Harry said, pointing.

Jake peered out towards the horizon but despite the fact that the moon was full and bright, he couldn't see a thing. 'What?'

'I can't quite tell. We need to get closer. If we

walk down to the end of the breakwater where the ice blocks get bigger, we can use them as stepping stones. Come on,' said Harry.

'I don't think I can jump that far,' said Jake, worried about falling into the icy water.

'I'll give you a piggyback part of the way. Here take my backpack.'

Jake knew it was incredibly stupid to walk on ice, but Harry *was* Super Soccer Boy, so he clambered on. Harry made a huge, super soccer leap on to the first ice block. With the weight of both boys on it, it was nearly submerged.

'I'm going to have to do this quickly or we'll sink,' said Harry. 'Hold on tight!'

Jake already was.

With the speed and skill of the fastest footballer ever born, Harry leapt from ice block to ice block, as if he were weaving his way through the Brazilian defence in the World Cup final.

After zig-zagging backwards and forwards, the blocks finally began to get a bit bigger and sturdier and he was able to slow down. Eventually, the gaps between the ice blocks were small enough for Harry to stop and drop off his passenger.

'Phew!' said Harry. 'You're going to have to stop eating so much!'

They carried on walking from one block to another. It was slippery though, and every now and then they fell over.

'I wish I'd brought my utility boots,' said Harry. Harry had designed himself some special football boots, especially for occasions like these.

'Look,' said Jake after a while. 'The ice is totally solid from here.'

Various bits and pieces were stuck in the ice. There were a couple of drinks cans that some scumbag must have left on the beach, lumps of seaweed and chunks of driftwood sticking up out of the frozen surface. There was even an inflatable dolphin!

Suddenly, Harry ducked down behind a piece of driftwood and pulled Jake down too. 'Shhh! I can hear something,' he said.

Jake got that fluttery feeling in his stomach that he always seemed to get at some point when he spent an evening investigating with Harry.

Now they could both see some things up ahead – some very strange things. There were a number of large structures arranged in a circle. They were about three metres tall and sort of conical in shape but with smooth sides, as if they'd been carved.

They were made of ice and were almost see-through – in fact you could only really see them because the moon was shining off the flat faces.

'What the . . .?' said Jake. 'It looks like Stonehenge, but the ice version.'

'That would be Icehenge then, surely,' said Harry.

'Ha ha, very funny! Hey, look at that!'

Each of the icy structures flashed in turn with a deep blue light. The light ran round the circle three times, then stopped.

'Whoa, that was kinda freaky,' whispered Jake.

'D'you know what?' said Harry. 'I think that's some sort of ring of defence.'

'Huh? Why? What for?'

'Not sure. They could be protecting something, or maybe they're some sort of warning signal or beacon. What if they weren't meteors at all last night, but alien spacecraft?'

'Oh come on, Harry, that's just mental,' said Jake, wishing he thought it was, but knowing it made some sort of sense, however far-fetched it sounded. 'Where are they then, these aliens?'

'Presumably,' said Harry tapping the ice with his foot, 'they're under here. Let's go closer.'

'Do we have to?' asked Jake. But he already knew the answer.

Chapter Seven

Close Encounters of the Icy Kind

Harry stood up and went slowly towards the ice structures with Jake close behind.

'No sudden movements, Jake,' he said.

Every few steps, he paused, keeping perfectly still whenever the sequence of lights flashed.

'What are we going to do when we get close to them?' Jake whispered.

'Dunno,' said Harry. 'We'll decide that when the time comes.'

Unfortunately, Jake was so intent on looking in front of him, that he hadn't noticed a lump of frozen seaweed sticking out of the ice.

'Oops!' Jake tried to keep his balance, but he slipped and slid around before crashing down hard on the ice, nose first. 'OUCH!'

'Oh dear,' said Harry.

'It's OK, I'm all right,' said Jake, touched at his friend's concern.

'No. Oh dear,' Harry said, pointing ahead.

All of the ice sentries were now flashing bright red.

'This does not look good,' said Harry, backing away.

The sentry nearest Jake shot a beam of light directly at him and began to make a whining sound.

'What's it doing, Harry?' asked Jake, nervously.

'I don't know, but I think we'd better move pretty quickly. Whatever they are, they've sensed we're here.'

Just as he finished speaking, a shard of ice shot out of the top of the sentry along the beam of light. It got Jake in the leg.

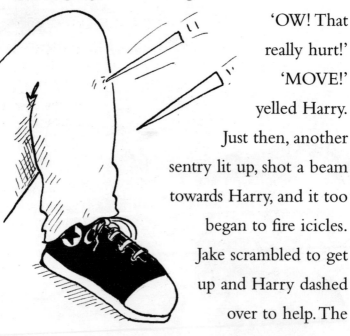

'OW! That really hurt!'

'MOVE!' yelled Harry. Just then, another sentry lit up, shot a beam towards Harry, and it too began to fire icicles. Jake scrambled to get up and Harry dashed over to help. The sentries continued to fire and it took all of Harry's super soccer skills to dive, dodge and kick away the sharp shards of ice, which seemed to get bigger and bigger. Jake had real problems and Harry was finding it impossible to protect him as well.

'OW! OUCH! That one went right through my jeans. Man, they're sharp!' Jake shouted.

Harry grabbed Jake's arm and pulled him to his feet. Ron briefly poked his head out of the backpack to see what was going on and just as quickly dived back in as an icicle flew between his ears.

'Get the football out of the backpack,' shouted Harry.

Jake fumbled it open and threw Harry the ball.

'I'll teach you to shoot at me!' Harry growled at the structures. He drop-kicked the ball with all his super soccer power at the sentry nearest to them.

It was a direct hit!

BOOF

The top of the sentry shattered into a million pieces and the beam of light went out.

'Woo-hoo! Shot, Harry!' cheered Jake.

The ball was deflected nearby and Harry went to pick it up, but as he did so, another two of the sentries aimed their beams at him and Jake. Harry managed to knock one more out with his next shot but the other sentry was still firing.

'Harry! HELP!' Jake called.

Then things got even weirder. A hole opened in the floor of the circle and a creature, which seemed to be made entirely of ice, appeared. The ice creature sped over to Jake as fast as lightning and breathed out little icicles all over him as he tried to get away.

Jake was beginning to panic. 'I'm getting covered in these shards! They're sticking in me all over the place.'

Harry was having enough trouble dodging the sentries. He managed to get over to Jake and grab him, booting the ice creature out of the

way. But when he looked over to the circle of sentries, he gasped in horror. 'Oh oh,' he said. From the hole, dozens of little ice creatures were pouring out and they were heading straight for Harry and Jake.

'Leg it!' shouted Jake.

'I'm doing my best!' said Harry. It wasn't easy to move quickly on the slippery ice. They managed to get a short distance away but the little icy creatures were too fast and soon they were swarming around him and Jake like ants around a jam doughnut. Jake was blue with cold, and couldn't do anything but shiver. Harry tried to escape but their icy breath was freezing his muscles. He dropped to his knees on the ice.

Harry gazed in awe as the hundreds of little ice creatures joined together to form one giant ice creature.

'Wow!' said Harry. He couldn't think of anything else to say.

HARRY, WHAT'S IT DOING?!

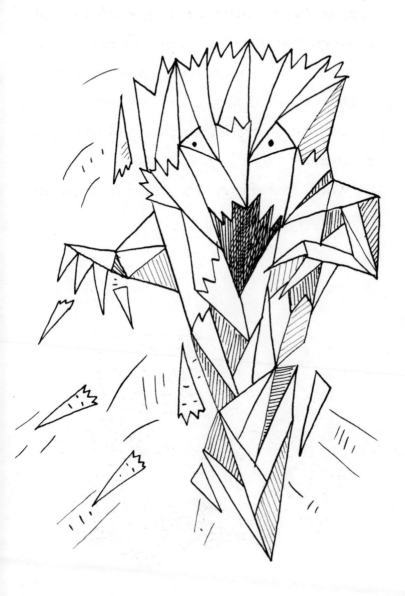

69

The creature bent down and picked them up, then carried them back to the circle of ice sentries, and down through the ice.

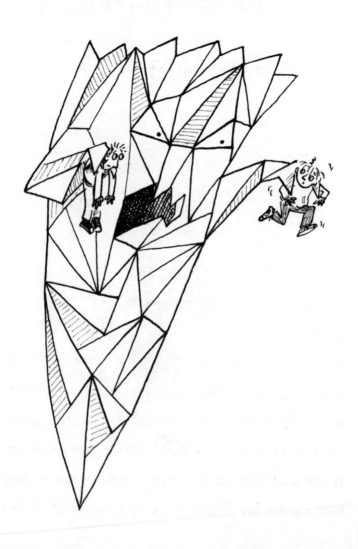

Chapter Eight

The Ziglons

Harry and Jake were placed in some sort of lift made of ice. The huge creature that had captured them split apart into hundreds of the small icy aliens and two of the aliens joined Harry and Jake in the lift. There were strange symbols on the lift's control panel that Harry guessed were in the aliens' language.

'How do they do that?' said Harry, awestruck.

'Do what?' said Jake, who was not feeling at all awestruck, just terrified.

'All join together. It's really amazing.'

Jake, however, was suffering too much from all the little bruises and pin pricks from the icicles to be amazed. He just felt sore and cold.

The lift descended deep below the surface, through the frozen sea, to where the alien creatures were obviously living.

'I wonder if this is a spaceship,' said Harry beginning to feel rather scared himself.

The lift stopped and they were taken along an icy corridor. Everything seemed to be made of ice. Harry remembered seeing an ice hotel on TV once, in Sweden he thought, and guessed it must be a bit like this. It was actually quite beautiful to look at despite the fact that he was scared of what was going to happen to them.

'You will wait here,' said one of the aliens, as

it pushed Harry and Jake into a room with walls

made of thick ice. The door slid closed behind them – there was no way out.

'I wonder how they can speak English,' said Harry.

'Yeah, it's odd, I hadn't thought of that,' said Jake shivering.

The door opened again and another alien handed them cloaks that looked as if they were made from snow.

'You will be cold here,' the alien said. 'Wear these. We use them to keep things at a constant

temperature. Your body heat will mean that they keep you warm.'

'Um, thanks,' said Harry, as he took the cloaks. They felt fluffy and not at all cold.

'I don't see how these can work,' said Jake, when the alien had left.

Harry put his on. 'Weird. You know this actually helps,' he said. 'Hopefully this is a good sign.'

'What, that we're imprisoned under the sea, in an icy cell having been attacked with shards of ice and captured by alien ice monsters?' asked

Jake, shakily, as he put his cloak on too.

'No,' said Harry calmly. 'That they've given us these to keep warm. Why would they do that if they wanted to hurt us?'

'Hmm,' said Jake.

About ten minutes later, a group of aliens came to the cell.

'You will come with us,' said one of them.

Harry and Jake were taken to a large room where an ice alien sat on a big throne-like seat.

'Greetings, Earthlings,' said the alien.

'I never thought I'd hear anyone say that in real life,' whispered Jake.

'Er, greetings, ice . . . er . . . creature,' said Harry.

The creature chuckled. 'We are Ziglons from planet Zog, human. And I am the Emperor.' His voice sounded sort of crispy and he spoke with an accent that reminded Jake of foreign films on TV.

'I'm Harry and this is Jake. How come you speak our language?' asked Harry.

'Simple, Earthling Harry. We have been observing your planet for some time,' said the Ziglon Emperor. 'We have been monitoring your broadcasts and have learnt all the most popular languages that you humans speak. We have watched many of your Earth programmes on what you call TV.

'This just gets weirder and weirder,' said Jake under his breath.

'We have been observing and studying a number of planets throughout the galaxy. We have been trying to find the closest and most suitable.'

'Suitable for what?' asked Harry, although he had a nasty feeling that he knew what the Emperor was going to say.

'For us to live on, of course. We have come to take over the Earth.'

Chapter Nine

The End of the World as We Know It

Harry and Jake looked at each other in horror.

'What do you mean?' said Harry finally.

'A-A-And what happens to us humans?!' Jake added.

'We are preparing your planet, or should I say,

our planet, for the rest of our people to settle here. Obviously Zog is much colder than what you call Earth. Your polar caps were what first attracted us to Earth. They are not as cold as our planet but they showed us that it had potential. From now we will call this planet Zog Beta.'

The creatures around him cheered.

'Our ships are here to prepare the planet with Zero Kelvinators,' continued the Emporor. 'These will lower the temperature and make it cold enough for us. It should take about ten years for the full changeover. By then, this planet will be an ice and rock planet just like Ziglon. It will be hard work but it will be worth it. At the moment, we need to spend most of the time under the sea in our spaceships as it's too warm outside. This is especially true during the daytime, so we prefer only to come out at night.'

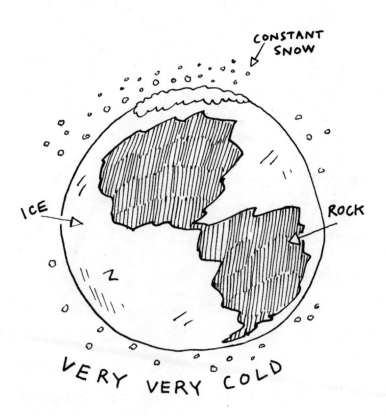

'But why are you doing this? You have a planet of your own,' said Harry. 'You're going to wipe out the entire human race and every living creature too!'

'Yes, that part is most regrettable, but a few humans may survive. As long as they leave us alone we will not harm them.'

Harry didn't know what to say. Jake had begun to blub, his tears freezing on his cheeks.

'I am really sorry but we have no choice. Let me explain,' the Ziglon Emperor said softly. 'You will understand we are not monsters.' He turned to one of the Ziglons nearby. 'Show them the latest transmission from home.'

A large screen embedded in the wall lit up. An

image formed and Harry and Jake saw what appeared to be another planet. It had a dark purple sky and what looked like three moons.

'This is our home planet, Zog.'

'It looks all right to me,' sniffed Jake.

'But there's no one around,' said Harry. 'The surface is deserted.'

'That is right, Earthling Harry, you speak the truth,' said the Emperor. 'Our sun grows bigger and hotter every day. The surface of Zog is no longer cold enough for us so we have been forced to live underground. Now that is becoming too warm, too, and those who venture onto the surface just melt.'

Harry and Jake could both see why being made of ice on a planet like that would be a problem.

'Ewwww!' said Jake. 'It must be horrible to melt.'

'Indeed, Earthling Jake, and this is why we must leave Zog – and why we must freeze your planet so that we can live here.'

'But couldn't you just do that on Zog?' asked Harry.

'I'm afraid not. The temperatures are too high already and are rising daily. As I said, our sun is growing larger because it is dying – this is what happens when a sun dies. We don't even know if Zog Beta will be ready before our planet becomes completely uninhabitable, but we have to try.' He looked very sad. 'We have searched for many of your decades and Earth is the only planet we have come across which is remotely suitable. I am very sorry.'

'This is hopeless,' said Jake. 'We have to get back and warn everybody.'

'That we cannot allow!' said the Ziglon Emperor, raising his voice and getting up from his throne.

'Me and my big mouth,' said Jake. 'Now we're for it.'

'Do not worry, Earthling Jake,' said the Emperor back at normal volume. 'We do not

want to hurt you. Our reason for capturing you was to protect ourselves from discovery. What will happen to your people will be a result of the change in climate. We do not intend to exterminate you directly.'

Jake and Harry didn't find that very reassuring.

'So you're letting us go then?' said Harry. 'But you must know we'll tell everyone about you.'

The Emperor smiled. 'There is just one thing we need to do before we take you back to the surface. You must go to the Hypno Pod.'

'The what?' asked Harry.

'The Hypno Pod. It will turn the events of this evening into a vague dreamlike memory. In your hypnotic state, you will be taken back to the beach and instructed to go back to your beds. We developed the technology on Zog and it has been tried on many alien species and has never failed. You will be the very first humans to experience it!' He glided over and shook their hands. 'It has been a pleasure to meet you both.' Then turning to some aliens he said, 'Take them away.'

Harry and Jake were led to a small, dark room. Inside was a sausage-shaped pod, made of some dark coloured ice. It had a little window near the top.

Harry desperately tried to think what he

could do. There were so many ice creatures around though, and even if he did manage to escape, he didn't think he would be able to get to the surface without the aliens' help.

'Who will be first?' asked the Ziglon in charge, and Harry realised it was too late to think of escape.

Harry took one look at Jake's pale face and stepped forward. 'Guess that'll be me,' he said, sounding more confident than he felt. 'It'll be OK, Jake.'

Well he hoped it would anyway.

Chapter Ten

Unforgettable?

As Harry was pushed into the pod, he concentrated hard on remembering every little detail about the last couple of hours, just as he would in a football game when he memorised every aspect of the pitch and the players.

'Just relax – this won't take long,' said the Ziglon. 'It won't hurt either.' The alien closed the door and fiddled with some knobs and dials.

Harry looked around the pod. It was filled with little coloured lights that twinkled in the icy walls and what looked like sensors everywhere. Suddenly he had an idea and took out his mobile phone and snapped a couple of photos, as a reminder – just in case. He couldn't really believe this little room would wipe his memory.

'Are you OK?' mouthed Jake from outside, looking really worried.

Harry gave Jake the thumbs up. Then there was a whooshing sound and the inside of the pod went completely dark.

Think. Think. Think, Harry told himself. It was over almost immediately and the door slowly opened. The Ziglon beckoned Harry out of the pod and stood Jake in his place.

'How are you feeling?' the alien asked Harry.

'I . . . who . . . what?' said Harry.

'Excellent!' said the Ziglon.

Jake looked horrified, but when the Ziglon turned its back, Harry winked at him. Then it was Jake's turn in the Hypno Pod.

Immediately afterwards, some aliens took Harry and Jake to the beach on ice scooters and left them to make their own way back to the hotel.

'Phew! That was a close one, wasn't it?' said Harry. 'I knew if I concentrated hard enough the Hypno Pod wouldn't work.'

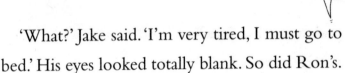

'What?' Jake said. 'I'm very tired, I must go to bed.' His eyes looked totally blank. So did Ron's.

'Jake! Jake!' said Harry, shaking him gently. 'Don't you remember where we've been?'

'What? We played football . . . I . . . Bed, I must go to bed.'

'Oh dear,' said Harry. 'Looks like the Hypno Pod worked on you. My super soccer powers must have protected me. Come on, let's go back to the hotel.'

Harry gently guided Jake up the hill to the hotel and then he tucked him into bed.

'Mmmm,' said Jake as he snuggled under the covers, sucking his thumb like a baby.

'Night, Jake. Sleep well. Though I don't think

that will be a problem,' said Harry. As he took Ron out of his backpack, he saw that the Ziglons had kindly returned his football.

Harry sat up, going over everything he'd seen, trying to remember each detail, but he just couldn't keep his eyes open, and very soon he was fast asleep.

The rest of Harry's night was filled with dreams of icy seas and giant Ziglons. He dreamt of a world of frozen football pitches and cancelled matches. It was not a good night. Not only that, but he was woken early by excited voices.

'I DON'T BELIEVE IT!' Eddie was shouting. 'It's snowing! Harry, Jake, Will, wake up! Look out of the window.'

Jake jumped out of bed. 'Awesome!' he said 'Snow in July!'

'I don't want to be a party pooper or anything, but surely that's not a good thing,' said Harry.

Eddie, Jake and Will looked at Harry.

'Er, I guess not,' said Will. His expression changed and he looked worried. 'D'you suppose it's something to do with global warming? I mean, my mum's always saying that the weather will get more extreme.'

'But snow in July can't count,' said Eddie. 'That's just wrong.'

'Jake,' said Harry, 'what do you think?' He was hoping the question might spark off a memory.

'Me . . . I . . . I've no idea. I had a really weird

dream though. You and I got captured by some aliens and they were the ones making it so cold.'

Will and Eddie laughed.

'Sounds like you must've kicked off your duvet in the night,' said Will.

'Yeah, or ate too much at dinner,' Eddie added.

'He always does!' they both said and fell about laughing.

There was a knock on the door.

'Meeting downstairs in fifteen minutes,' said Mr Blunt.

'Let's go out in the snow before it melts,' said Will.

'Yeah, we can have a snowball fight. And I've got to get some pictures with my phone – my mum will never believe this!' Eddie said.

They got dressed in less than a minute, putting on as many layers as possible, and dashed downstairs. Jake was staring out of the window.

'It felt so real, my dream,' he said quietly.

'Jake,' said Harry, 'you do realise that it wasn't a dream? It actually happened.'

Jake looked at Harry in disbelief. 'Don't be daft, Harry.'

'Really, Jake. I was there! We were under the

ice in an alien spaceship. They showed us what was happening on their planet.'

'How did you know that was in my dream? I never said!'

'I told you, it wasn't a dream! They're called Ziglons and they put us both into a Hypno Pod so we wouldn't remember. It didn't work on me though. Hang on a moment.' Harry suddenly remembered his phone. He ran and grabbed it from his hoody. 'Look! I took some pictures inside the Hypno Pod.'

Jake took the phone and scrolled through the photos. In one of them he could see himself in the background.

'But . . . I . . . I . . .' he stuttered.

'Yes, I know, you don't remember.'

Jake sat down with a thump.

'We have to decide what we're going to do about the Ziglons,' said Harry. 'And fast, before we all freeze to death.'

This was a job for Super Soccer Boy!

Chapter Eleven

The Big Freeze

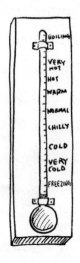

Harry and Jake joined the others in the TV room. Now Jake believed what Harry had told him, he was trying hard to remember it all for himself. But there was more bad news on the way.

'OK, everyone,' said Mr Blunt. 'As you can see, there have been several centimetres of snowfall overnight and I'm afraid all of the pitches are frozen, so all of the matches have been cancelled.'

There was a collective 'oh' of disappointment from the whole team.

'We will, of course have another look at lunchtime to see if the pitches are playable for the afternoon games, but it's not looking very likely. If they're cancelled too, and if they remain frozen tomorrow, the organisers are saying that the tournament will be abandoned.'

The whole team gasped. They knew the Middletown Mini-Stars had a good chance of

winning, especially with Harry in the team. They all wanted a winner's medal to take home.

'But we don't care if it's cold,' said Will.

'Health and safety, lad. If the ground's frozen, it's too dangerous,' explained Mr Blunt. 'This just gets worse and worse,' said Harry. 'I've also had some phone calls from worried parents,' Mr Blunt continued. 'None of you came prepared for this sort of weather – you only have summer clothes, so they want you to stay in the hotel where it's warm, unless you're playing football.'

'But we were making a giant snowman,' said Sanjay. His clothes were wet and his teeth were chattering from being in the cold for too long.

'Well, I'm responsible for you lot and I'm telling you to stay inside,' said Mr Blunt.

'That's boooring,' moaned Will.

'It gets worse, I'm afraid,' said Mr Blunt. 'If the weather doesn't change tomorrow we'll probably have to go home.'

'WHAT!' they cried all together. 'That's not fair!'

'But we were supposed to stay all week!' said Eddie.

'Why can't we stay and play in the snow?' said Sanjay.

Harry left them all complaining and went into the lounge and turned on the TV. He found the news channel, hoping for a report on what was going on around Puddletown. He wasn't disappointed. There was a reporter wrapped head to toe in ski gear. A strong wind gusted about her and snow blew across the screen.

'Here I am in Puddletown-on-Sea, or should I say Puddletown-on-Ice,' she shouted above the howling wind. 'As you can see, the sea is now completely frozen. Experts are baffled as to what is causing the freeze. But concern is mounting as the ice continues to spread along the coast.' She paused for maximum dramatic effect. 'Where will it stop?'

★ ★ ★

Meanwhile in the Ziglon spaceship below the sea, everything seemed to be running smoothly.

The snow outside was getting thicker and thicker. Harry and Jake sat in their hotel room, wrapped in their duvets to keep themselves warm. Ron was curled up in one of Harry's football socks. They needed somewhere private to talk.

'What are we going to do, Harry?' said Jake. 'It's happening so fast.'

'I don't know,' said Harry. 'If we can't get the Ziglons to stop we'll have to persuade them to leave. But I don't think they will – they're pretty desperate.'

Lunchtime came and went (Mrs Plunkett had asked the cook to make a nice warming winter stew) and the boys huddled around the TV once more – there was nothing else to do. A very serious-looking newsreader appeared on the screen.

'It is now dangerously cold in Puddletown, so our reporter has been forced to set up a remote web cam on the promenade to observe the area.'

The TV cut to a view of . . . not very much. All you could see was ice and snow.

'Professor Winklestein, you've been watching these strange events right from the start. The question we all want to ask is this: Are we entering a new ice age?'

'Well,' said the professor, 'I can see why you would think that. Let me show you our solar system.' He pointed to a model with the sun in the centre. 'Here's Earth and here are the planets that are closest to us – that's Mercury and Mars. Beyond these are the outer planets: Jupiter, Saturn, Uranus, Neptune and little Pluto which is so far from the sun it is really just a little icy rock. What we —'

But Harry never found out what the professor was going to say. He leapt from his chair. 'That's it!' he shouted.

He grabbed Jake and dragged him out of the room, leaving the others to wonder what Harry was so excited about.

'What's the hurry, Harry?' asked Jake.

'I know what to do!' said Harry. 'Quick, wrap up as warm as you can. We're going down to the sea.'

Chapter Twelve

Return to the Ice

They sped upstairs and dressed in as many layers
of clothes as they had.

'I'm going to need these,' said Harry putting
on his utility boots. 'And this.' He picked up the
backpack which still had the football in it. 'We'd

better not go out the front – Mr Blunt might catch us.' He opened the window. Freezing air and a flurry of snow blew into the room. 'You stay here, Ron, or you'll freeze.'

For once Ron was happy to stay behind.

'It's the second floor, Harry,' said Jake nervously.

'It's OK, I can give you a piggyback. My boots will get us down safely.' Harry switched them to hover mode and climbed out of the window. 'Hop on,' he said.

As soon as Jake was on Harry's back, he shut his eyes tight.

'Next stop, ground floor,' said Harry and gently floated down.

Puddletown looked like a scene from a Christmas card.

'Wow!' Jake said, looking around.

'Come on, there's no time to lose,' said Harry charging off.

'But what's the plan?' asked Jake.

'I'll tell you on the way,' Harry answered. 'Grab a lid,' he added as they passed the dustbins.

'Grab a what?' said Jake

'A dustbin lid,' said Harry.

Jake looked at Harry as if he'd gone bonkers, but he did as he was told.

Five minutes later they stood on the snow-covered beach, looking at the sheet of ice which had once been the sea. Harry had told Jake what he intended to do.

'Do you really think they'll go for it?' asked Jake.

'No idea, but it's worth a try. I'm going to skate across so hop on – you'll need another piggyback. Here we go!' He pressed the *skates* button on his utility boot remote control and two blades projected from the bottom of the boots.

Harry sped off. He was like one of those speed skaters you see in the winter Olympics, except without the silly outfit – and the frozen sea was also a bit bumpy. Harry had to fight against the wind and dodge in and out of the obstacles in the ice with super soccer speed.

Before they knew it, they reached the sentries, and gasped.

Now there were three times as many ice
sentries on guard!

Harry stopped and Jake got down.

'OK,' said Harry. 'Just move forward slowly . . .
I don't think they're going to be particularly
happy to see us.'

Harry was right. They'd only taken a couple
of steps when the sentries lit up and started
shooting icy shards.

'Use the lids,'
yelled Harry.
Jake and Harry
raised the
bin lids

like shields, and the icicles bounced off them. That's what he'd wanted them for!

But more sentries started firing, and before long there were so many that Harry and Jake were pinned to the spot.

In the spaceship below, the Ziglons watched them crouching behind the dustbin lids.

'It's those Earthling boys that were here yesterday, your majesty,' said Blurg.

'I thought they were put in the Hypno Pod,' the Emperor replied, angrily.

'They were!'

'Then what are they doing back here?!'

'I don't know, maybe . . . Look!'

They peered at the monitor. Harry, using his

bin lid as protection from the ice shards, was skating around in a very strange way. He was darting here, there and everywhere.

'He's carving a message in the ice,' said the Emperor, amazed. 'How odd!'

PLEASE LET US IN WE WANT TO TALK TO YOU

'Should we blast them with the freeze ray from the cannons, your majesty?'

'No! I want to hear what they have to say. It must be important for them to risk coming back in the freezing cold.'

'But what if it's a trick?' said Blurg.

'I said let them in!' said the Emperor.

Much to Harry and Jake's relief, the shards of ice suddenly stopped. Two Ziglons came up through the ice and escorted them down in the lift, and to the Emperor. Harry bowed – it seemed like a good idea to be extra polite. Jake followed his lead.

'Your majesty,' Harry began. 'Thank you for allowing us to see you.'

'I hope you have a very good reason for being here,' said the Ziglon Emperor. 'I want to know why the Hypno Pod didn't work. It always has before.' He was clearly not exactly pleased to see them.

'It worked on me,' said Jake, still finding it hard to believe that he was actually talking to an alien. 'But Harry's, sort of, well, special. I mean he's Super Soccer Boy. He has all these amazing skills. It just didn't work on him.'

The Emperor raised his icy eyebrows. Then he frowned menacingly and shouted so loud it made them both put their hands over their ears as his icy voice seemed to echo in their heads. 'YOU SHOULD NEVER HAVE COME BACK! NOW YOU WILL HAVE TO BE DESTROYED!'

Harry stepped forward bravely. 'But we had to,' he said. 'What you're doing – freezing Earth – it's just not right.'

'SILENCE!' shouted the Emperor again. 'I have told you we have no choice. I am the

Emperor of Zog and you will not stop me from saving my people. Take these humans away and freeze them!'

'But what if there was an alternative?' said Harry quickly, as the aliens started to lead them away. 'There's a dark, icy, rock planet really near, where no one lives.'

'There is no such place!' said the Emperor angrily.

'But there is!' said Harry and went on before the Emperor could interrupt again. 'It's called Pluto. It's right on the edge of our solar system and it's very small. It's not really a planet at all so you might have mistaken it for an asteroid, but it orbits our sun just like the Earth does. And it would be cold enough for you and the rest of your people right now! It's at least ten times colder than our polar caps. You could move there immediately – no ten-year wait.'

'Blurg!' called the Emperor to one of the aliens. 'Find Pluto and bring it up on the screen.'

Blurg brought the solar system up on the screen. He zoomed in on Pluto.

'He's right you know,' said Blurg, after a while, analysing the data. 'No atmosphere, dark, cold, icy —'

They all stared at the desolate rocky landscape on the screen

'What is the current surface temperature?' the Emperor asked.

'It is currently, erm, minus 230 degrees celsius,' said Blurg.

Jake shivered.

'What do you think?' said the Emperor.

'Well,' said Blurg, tapping his keyboard. 'To reduce the temperature on Earth to this level would take more than ten years. In that time life on Zog would probably no longer exist. We could actually go to this Pluto and adapt it within months.'

The Emperor asked more and more questions. Eventually Harry realised that his expression had changed to one of relief.

'Well, young Earthling!' he said, finally. 'It looks like you've saved your planet!'

'He's always doing that,' said Jake proudly.

'Erm ... I don't want to sound rude, but how quickly can you go?' said Harry.

'Blurg, how long will it take to prepare the ships for take off?' asked the Emperor.

'Hmmm. We need to disconnect the Zero Kelvinators, inform planet Zog so that they can prepare to join us and charge the engines. I would say about two and a half Earth hours.'

'I don't suppose you know how long it will take for the ice to melt and the weather to get back to normal?' asked Harry.

'Well, the charging and blast off of the

engines will start the melting process, and being the middle of your summer, it should be well on its way by morning,' Blurg replied.

'Sweet!' said Harry.

The Emperor became positively friendly all of a sudden. 'Well, boys,' he said. 'How would you like a quick tour of our spaceship while everything is prepared? Then we will take you back to shore before blast off. You wouldn't want to get caught in that!'

As they were looking round the spaceship, the Emperor said, 'Tell us some more about this game of football that you all play, and that you are so good at. It sounds most interesting.'

Jake taught some of the Ziglons football techniques, while Harry desmonstrated them, and before long, they were all having a kickabout!

Two hours later, Harry and Jake were taken back to the beach on ice scooters by some exhausted aliens! Even the Emperor went along to say goodbye.

Harry took his football out of the backpack and handed it to the Emperor.

'Here,' he said. 'I'd like you to take the football with you. Maybe you can start a league of your own on Pluto.'

'Thank you, Earthling Harry!' said the Emperor. 'But I think now you should call it Zog Beta!'

Harry and Jake stood on the beach and waved as the Ziglons went back to their ship.

'Let's wait and watch them take off,' said Harry.

'Have to,' agreed Jake. 'Don't think we'll get to meet many more aliens!'

Just then, there was a huge rumbling, followed by an enormous crack as the spaceships rose out of the ice.

They hovered about a bit, the flames flaring out. It was spectacular to watch. Blue sparks rained down onto the ice and twinkled and died. Then spouts of water began to shoot up through holes in the ice like huge fountains. The sea bubbled as if it was boiling, as the pressure from below was released. Surprised-looking fish shot into the air before plopping back down into the sea.

Then, one by one, the spaceships rose high into the sky, and disappeared off into space, flying in formation.

'There they go!' said Harry. 'I hope they're happy in their new home.'

'Hey! Harry, look out!' shouted Jake. A huge wave was coming towards them.

'Oops!' said Harry. He grabbed Jake and sped off just in time so they didn't get soaked. 'Looks like the thaw is well under way!'

Chapter Fourteen

End Game

It was. In fact, by the next morning it had warmed up enough for the tournament to carry on, which was what Harry had hoped all along.

The Middletown Mini-Stars thrashed everyone and at the end of the tournament,

Harry got the Golden Boot for most goals scored. Nobody ever knew that he'd saved the planet too, except Jake and Ron of course. But the thing that made Harry feel proudest of all was the fact that far away on another planet, aliens would soon be playing football.

Have you read these Super Soccer Boy books?

Super Soccer Boy
and the Exploding Footballs

Super Soccer Boy
and the Evil Electronic Bunnies

Super Soccer Boy
and the Snot Monsters

Super Soccer Boy
and the Attack of the Giant Slugs

Coming Soon:

Super Soccer Boy
and the Laser Ray Robbery

Super Soccer Boy
and the Raging Robots

HARRY'S F⚽⚽TBALL FACTS!

In 1973 an Italian referee was taken to hospital after being bitten on the back by an angry player.

In 1954 Turkey beat Spain in a World Cup qualifier by drawing straws. A blindfolded Italian boy picked the straws to decide the winner.

Jean Langenus of Belgium refereed the 1930 World Cup final. He wore a suit jacket, stripy red tie and golfing plus fours.

In 1908 soccer was made an Olympic event.

An experiment to use two referees was trialled in 1935.

JOE PAYNE

of Luton Town is the only player to score 10 goals in a football league match. He did it on 13th April 1936.

It's said that football was actually invented in CHINA. It was written about in around 476 BC and was called 'Cuju'.

The famous English club Aston Villa was founded by the Wesleyan Chapel cricket team in 1874. They wanted to keep fit in the winter.

In 1998, an English referee sent himself off after punching a player during a Sunday League game...

...and in 1968 on Nov 8th, in a third division match between Barrow + Plymouth Argyle, the referee deflected the ball, accidentally scoring the only goal.

Join
Super Soccer Boy
online:

www.supersoccerboy.com

⚽ Fun activities
⚽ Football facts and quiz
⚽ All the latest
on the books
⚽ And much more!